STICKNEY-FOREST VIEW LIBRARY DISTRICT

W9-BMY-973

Copyright © 2021 Clavis Publishing Inc., New York

Originally published as *Theo's prinses* in Belgium and the Netherlands by Clavis Uitgeverij, 2020

Visit us on the Web at www.clavis-publishing.com.

No part of this publication may be reproduced or stored in a retrieval system, or transmitted in any form or by any means, electronic, mechanical, photocopying, recording, or otherwise, without the prior written permission of the publisher, except in the case of brief quotations embodied in critical articles and reviews.
For information regarding permissions, write to Clavis Publishing, info-US@clavisbooks.com.

Theo's Princess written by Ellen DeLange and illustrated by Monty Lee

ISBN 978-1-60537-640-0

This book was printed in December 2020 at Nikara, M. R. Štefánika 858/25, 963 01 Krupina, Slovakia.

First Edition
10 9 8 7 6 5 4 3 2 1

Clavis Publishing supports the First Amendment and celebrates the right to read.

THEO'S
princess

Clavis
NEW YORK

Written by Ellen DeLange
Illustrated by Monty Lee

Once upon a time there was a frog named Theo.
Well, his name was actually Theodore Cornelius Baffelus III.

Although he had a very noble name,
when he looked at his reflection in the pond,
he only saw an ordinary green frog without a crown . . .

Growing up, Theo had always heard stories about a princess who, with a single kiss, turned a frog into a prince.
He wished that one day he too would turn into a prince.

Theo knew it wouldn't be easy to become a prince.
First of all, he had to find a princess, who then had
to like him enough to kiss him.

Even the thought of being kissed made him blush a little.
He felt nervous about finding a princess, but was up for the challenge.
After all, this was his only chance to become a prince.

When Theo arrived at the palace gate,
he tried to get around the guards,
but they spotted him and chased him away.
"I will try my luck elsewhere," he thought.

In town, he smelled the sweet scent of cinnamon buns.
He took a peek inside the bakery.
"Could there be a princess here?" Theo asked himself.

But he only saw the baker and his son busy
kneading bread. "Where can I possibly
find a princess?" he wondered.

He hopped down the street.
When he arrived at a beautiful house,
he climbed on the windowsill to take a look inside.
There he saw a pretty maiden,
wearing an apron decorated with crowns.

"Could *she* be a princess?" he wondered.
Then someone entered into the kitchen
and kissed her on the cheek.
"Hmmm, no princess for me here either,"
sighed Theo.

Then he came across a beauty salon.
"Maybe I'll find my princess here, the daughter of a beauty Queen . . ."

He hopped inside, but as soon as
the women saw him, they screamed.
Startled, Theo ran out the door.

He expanded his search for a princess and travelled far and wide.

After a while, he came back home completely exhausted and still without a princess.

Theo knew he had to come up with another idea.
He grabbed some paper and started cutting, drawing, and writing.
Paper flew all over the place!

When he was finished, he admired his work.

He went outside to stick his carefully crafted posters everywhere.

On the day as advertised on the poster,
Theo arrived very early at the market square.
He looked around nervously.
"Will any princesses show up?" he wondered.

Theo waited and waited, but still no princesses.
"Are there still princesses out there?" he mused.
"Or do they only exist in bedtime stories?"

All of a sudden, he saw princesses coming from every corner.
Theo was so relieved. They had apparently read his call,
and were forming a long line!

Theo climbed on top of a soap box, cleared his throat, and shouted:
"Good day, I'm so excited that you have come to this special occasion!
Shall we start?"

The princesses were giggling.
They had never kissed a frog before.
One by one they came forward
and gave Theo a kiss.

After every kiss, Theo anxiously waited for something to happen.
Time and time again he looked in the mirror, but still saw a frog.
"How long will it take before I turn into a prince?" he wondered.

Suddenly there was turmoil. One of the princesses had fainted.
"I didn't know that I had to kiss a real frog!" she sobbed.

Theo had almost reached the end of the line. He thought it was wonderful
that all those princesses had come especially for him.
Unfortunately, he had not yet changed into a prince.
He was still the same frog . . .

Theo gave up hope. He felt sad and
slowly turned around to go home.
"Wait!" a small voice called out.
And before he knew it, a beautiful frog
stepped forward and gave him a big kiss.

Theo was baffled. Where did she come from?
Was she even a princess?
Wait, what was happening?

He felt butterflies in his stomach and his cheeks slowly turned red.
Would he change into a prince after all?
Theo could barely speak. "Whhoo a-are you?" he stammered.

"I'm Sofia. I may not be a princess, but when I saw your call, I thought:
what a handsome frog!" she said shyly. "That's why I came."
Theo fell in love instantly, forgetting all about becoming a prince.

Although Theo may not have turned into a real prince, he felt like one,
now that he had found his princess. They looked at each other and
knew they would live happily ever after.